An Old Shell

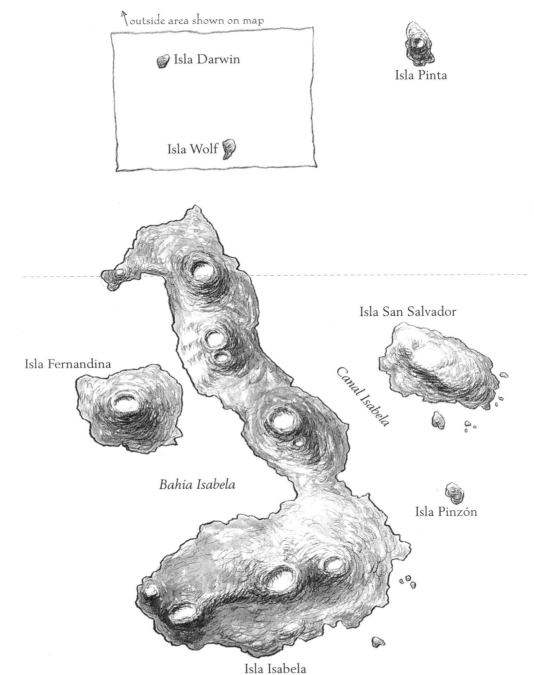

outside area shown on map

Isla Darwin

Isla Wolf

Isla Pinta

Isla San Salvador

Isla Fernandina

Canal Isabela

Bahía Isabela

Isla Pinzón

Isla Isabela

Pacific Ocean

Archipiélago de Colón ～ Galápagos Islands

Isla Marchena

Isla Genovesa

Equator

Isla Baltra

Isla Santa Cruz

Isla Santa Fé

Isla San Cristóbal

Isla Santa María

Isla Española

TONY JOHNSTON

An Old Shell

POEMS OF THE GALÁPAGOS

Pictures by TOM POHRT

Farrar Straus Giroux
New York

For Ernesto Vaca Norero and Barry Boyce

And for my shipmates on the Galápagos voyage: Richard Benz;
Lars, Marlies, Nils, and Sonja Bjork; Nancy Contolini; Walter Hintz;
Ashley, Jenny, Samantha, and Roger Johnston; Joseph Lapiana;
Susan Nordyke; Carolyn Staudt; and Jill Strauss

With thanks to the Charles Darwin Foundation for its ongoing efforts to protect and
preserve the irreplaceable Galápagos Islands. For further information please write to:
Charles Darwin Foundation, Inc.
100 North Washington Street, Suite 311
Falls Church, VA 22046

Text copyright © 1999 by Tony Johnston. Illustrations copyright © 1999 by Tom Pohrt
All rights reserved. Distributed in Canada by Douglas & McIntyre Ltd.
Printed and bound in the United States of America. Designed by Filomena Tuosto
First edition, 1999

Library of Congress Cataloging-in-Publication Data
Johnston, Tony, date.
    An old shell : poems of the Galápagos / Tony Johnston ; pictures by Tom Pohrt. — 1st ed.
        p. cm.
    Summary: A collection of poems exploring and celebrating the Galápagos Islands and their
various animals, including "The Voyage of the Rice Rat," "Magnificent Frigatebird," and "The Sea
Lion's Song."
    ISBN 0-374-35649-1
    1. Galápagos Islands—Juvenile poetry. 2. Children's poetry, American. [1. Galápagos Islands—
Poetry. 2. Animals—Poetry. 3. American poetry.] I. Pohrt, Tom, ill. II. Title.
PS3560.0393043   1999
811'.54—dc21   98-3212

The natural history of this archipelago is very remarkable:
it seems to be a little world within itself;
the greater number of its inhabitants,
both vegetable and animal,
being found nowhere else.
— Charles Darwin, *Voyage of the* Beagle

For every thing that lives is Holy.
—William Blake, *The Marriage of Heaven and Hell*

CONTENTS

An Old Shell

The Sea Is Our Mother

The sea is our mother
rocking,
rocking.
See how she fills
her blue arms
with gifts—
slippery bits of
weed,
white
shells,
fish
as bright as
wisps
of moon.
Hear how her voice
lifts,
falls,
lifts
while she sings our
life.

The Birth of Fernandina Island

One molten morning
the world
                    explodes
in sprays of sparks,
plumes of smoke,
gush
        of lava,
                water,
                        ash
spitting,
        spurting,
                spewing
from the sea's crucible
with a great hiss
to make this terrible
    barnacle.

Moment

On a bare branch, one
iguana sits, still and dark
against the dawn.

Isabela Island's Story

Last night a whale
    went gliding by
        in huge and barnacled
        glory.
I felt her
    gentle nudge
        against
          my shore.
If I could speak
    like surf, or gulls,
        this would be my
        story—
A wandering whale touched me
    last night.
        Last night I touched
        a whale.

Beetle

Out of dimness dawns the day.
A beetle creeps over the lava
    rubble—
one dark gleam,
one perfect polished pebble
feeling its way along the rim
    of morning—
simply being
        a beetle.

The Voyage of the Rice Rat

I heard of islands in the sea.
I heard it on the wind.
On tangled vines I drifted off.
I left all land behind.

I heard of islands in the blue.
I heard it on the waves
that swelled and swirled and swashed and swam
around me night and day.

I felt as lonely as the sea
that reaches for a shore,
as lonely as the old white moon
that roams the old white stars.

I dreamed of islands wild and green.
I dreamed of touching land.
I dreamed and floated on and on
the ocean without end.

I knew of islands—close, oh, close.
I knew it from a gull.
Its raspy, rowdy, raucous squawk
broke the water's spell.

I walked on islands warm with sun.
I lay down in the sand
and heard a soft salt-whisper, *"Home."*
I heard it on the wind.

Galápagos Rail

The tiny rail is loath to fly.
It sticks close to the ground
and seeks out insects. It is shy.
The tiny rail is loath to fly.
For succulent arachnidae,
it probes the leafy mounds.
The tiny rail is loath to fly.
It sticks close to the ground.

Greater Flamingo

Pale as the pink lip
of a shell, it drinks from its
cool green reflection.

Nesting, Genovesa Island

Watch the white petals
of fluttering gulls brush the
stone face of the cliff.

Flightless Cormorant

Clumsy withered feather-stubs
have beached this strange dark child.
But in his dreams he spreads great wings
and glides the ocean wild.

The Gull's Wish

Give me a guano island
bound by the sound
of the sea.
Any spot of rock
washed with white
will do.
Show me a small outcropping,
built from droppings, slow,
that grew
         and grew—
a dot where I can go
to rest
      my wings,
a lump of bird lime
like a green sea turtle's hump,
drenched with the fragrant
  stench
of time,
alive with vagrant gulls
crying news
from far
        and far.

A shining guano island.
That is my desire.

Magnificent Frigatebird

The frigatebird knows
what it is to swallow
   fire,
to fly
with its throat aflame,
   then float
in the blue—
a minor sun
caught in its own
         glow.

Rain, Española

Over the island
clouds drift
on their dark still wings.
Silver beaks
of rain
come softly pecking
at the cliff.

Painted Locust

To the hawk and the dove,
those who soar high above,
give the grand house of sky
and wind-breath.

But for me save a place
in the weeds. A small space.
I like it here close
to the earth.

Small White Flowers

At night the lava cactus blooms
In small white flowers. Its faint perfume
Floats upon the quiet dark
Along the lava still and stark
Where lone owl, old cold shadow, glides
While rice rat hugs the dark and hides.
When dawn comes up and darkness goes
Silently the petals close.
No one sees them in the gloom,
Small white flowers to please the moon.

Sally Lightfoot Crab

Who was Sally Lightfoot?
A green-island
   dancer?
Someone's great-grandmother?
                    A queen
torn from her African
   home?
Each time I see her namesake
come quick-stepping
   the
      high
         tide,
come skibbling over the sand
  in
      delicate
         dressage,
I thank her
for the gift she left—
  her
     lithe
       and
         lively
           name.

Galápagos Penguins

The penguins are swimming
                    again.
See how the water
    holds them
in its cool green
                    hands,
how it lifts them
light as kelp
lets them splash
    and reel
        and roll
over its bright
    back.
Oh, see how the water
    loves them!

Black Turtle Cove

In dawn's
silver

mangrove trees lean
close to

the sleeping
water

and listen to turtles
whisper.

Plankton

Have you ever considered the plankton
that moves in thick
streams
through deep
    water?

It teems with tiny wanderers—
minute Odysseuses—
shrimp- and crab-like things,
water fleas, worms,
and diatoms.

All day, all night
they float,
small boats
    adrift
in rippling ribbons
of life
                    until—
whales swallow them.
Until they become
                    whales.

Have you ever considered the plankton?

The Whale

Dawn.
Gray and pale and still,
like the first dawn,
like the Beginning.
Through the water a whale comes
swimming a gleaming
swath of calm.
An old old whale.

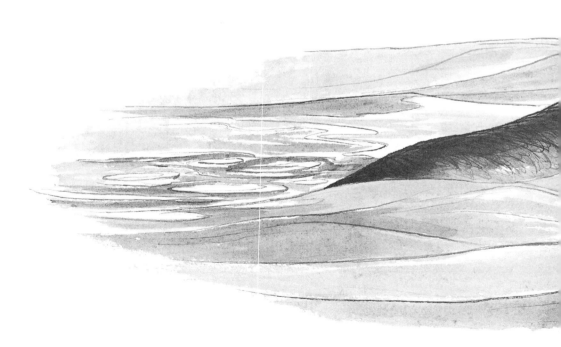

Suddenly it breaks
   the surface,
shatters the foam,
                rises
gray and pale and full
   of light,
like a great piece of
   dawn,
like part of the
Beginning.

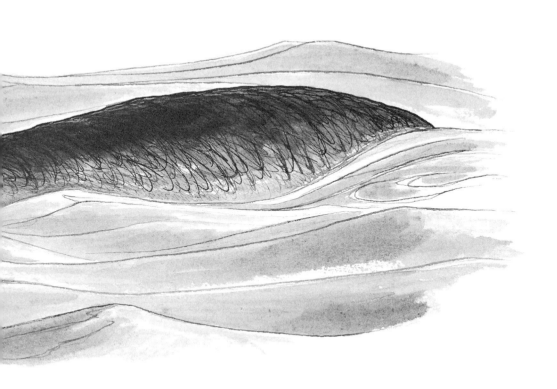

Sea Lion

The shining boulder
silken with sea
heaves itself
onto the beach
then
sleeps
  and sleeps
    and sleeps
steeping in sun
soaking up sun
storing sun
   until
completely and utterly
  warm
it plunges
back into the
   foam.

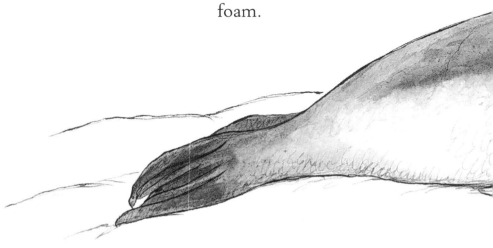

The Sea Lion's Song

Look. I have found the wreck
  of a sea lion,
its bones strewn on the shore
like a cargo of
  small white flutes.

I pick one up,
raise it to my lips
and pipe
  the sea lion's

        song.

The Ghost

At the edge of the world
a strange creature
    floats
        in mist.
Closer it comes
bobbing like a
  shell.
Close.
      Close.
It nears.
It is a boat,
sails bellied out
by the wind's salt
         breath.
Its great hull swells
like the breast
of a great
      gull.
Now it is here,
this boat of mist—
come again—
the *Beagle*.
    What will it find upon the shore?
      What will still be left?
        What forever lost?

Land Iguana

Swarthy little pile
of pebbled skin
    and blink
he is the most utterly ugly
    thing
on earth
and useless
except to sleep
on a rock
       sunning
or graze on prickly pear.

His life is as dear
      as any.

The Voice

A sound is slanting on the hills.
It spills through tree and weed and bush.
It pools in mountains tall and green
And still. It is the water's voice.
An ancient voice, an urgent voice
As old as dark, as old as dawn,
It lifts and calls the tortoise forth.
Its coolness whispers *Come. Oh, come.*

The tortoise hears inside its old
Head, the water beckoning,
Unerring knows the path to climb.
It needs no other reckoning.
A deep-sleep walker, up it plods,
Up to the brimming seeps of rain.
It gulps the gleaming water, then
Lumbers slowly down again.

The slow years ebb, the slow years flow.
The water calls; the tortoise goes.

Buccaneers

They came one day and saw
the tortoises,
some one century old.
With hooked hands
they took them
    and sailed
        and sailed.

They came at noon and took
the tortoises
asleep in the sun,
heaved them down
into the dark hold
    then sailed
        and sailed.

Deep in the hold they heard
the tortoises
scratch—
slow centuries piled.
They ate them.
Into the sea they heaved
their bones
    then sailed
        and sailed
            away.

The Iguanas of Santiago

Once they roamed
these lava flows
                as I do.
They heard the beat
of waves
that break the rocks,
felt the damp
garúa.
        As I do
they loved
cactus blooms.
The iguanas saw
the sun rise
  every day.
Like me, they knew
the white clear
                moon.
Here I stand.
The iguanas
            are
                gone.

Green Turtle

A turtle leaves the sea and climbs a dune.
She lays her eggs (as white as any moon),
While a hawk is circling, silent as a ghost,
While the wind goes whistling, *Everything is risk*.

One night the hatchlings split their moon-white husks
And scuttle to the endless sea at last,
Where the shark is waiting, swimming silent rings,
Where the waves are whispering, *Risk is everything*.

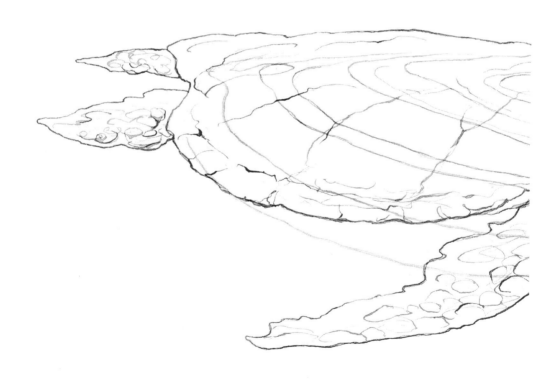

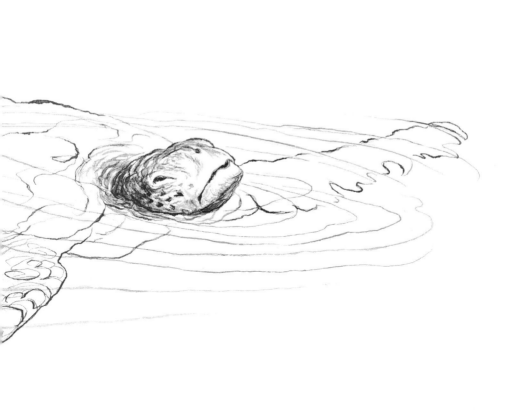

Sea Cucumbers

Over
   and over
     and over
      and over
the old waves curl
   upon each other,
     long salt-gleams
      that reach forever.
All the while
   beneath the water
     divers pluck
      from dark rock chambers
slow still poems—
   sea cucumbers.
     Soon these small lives
      quickly plundered
will be gone,
   will only linger
     in the memory
      of the water
that over
   and over
     and over
      and over
       rolls away
        —away forever.

Long-horned Grasshoppers

And now the great crepuscular choir
comes singing.
Every bush throbs with its
   hymn
of stars
of dreams
of wings.

I know the words
   by heart
so now
      I sing.

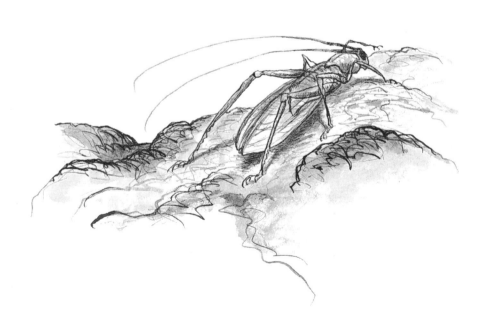

Pacific

Shimmering in her silver
  skin
she stretches to where the sky
comes down
and sings
      and sings.

So many suns
have drowned here.
So many more suns
         will.

The Dream

I dreamed that it was moonrise
and the sea was silver.
All the animals stood shining
on the shore
—dark-billed cuckoo, beetle, tortoise, plover—
for one moment held in stillness
all together.
When I came close
they slipped away
into the silver
water.

Listen

Listen.
A finch is singing,
trilling
     its joy
to the sky
all day.

In time,
when this island
   slumps
into the sea
where it began,
somewhere above
the finch's song
      will stay.

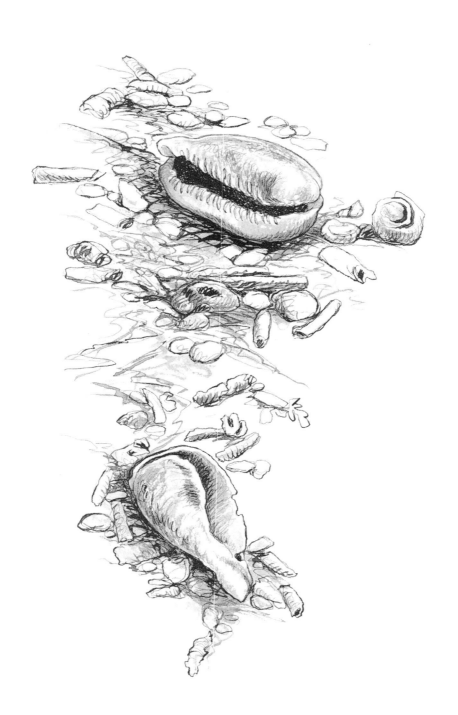

Galápagos

Hold this place
   gently
like an old shell.
Hold it
to your ear.
Hear the song that sings
                        inside—
     splash of fish
     flutter of finch
     rustle of salt
       wind
     lava hissing
     in wet sand
     and the echo of loneliness
       wild and wide.

Listen.
Hold it close.
Then let it slide
back into the hand
of the tide.

The Galápagos Islands lie six hundred miles off the western coast of South America. There are thirteen major islands, six minor ones, and many islets. For centuries, millenniums, they rose from the Pacific like the dark backs of sea turtles. They lay there unknown except to insects, birds, seeds, and a few animals thought to have reached their shores on vegetation "rafts" drifted from the mainland—untouched except by sun and wind and waves. Because of their isolation, species developed on each island, distinct from any other, distinct from anywhere else on earth.

Once man came upon them, probably in the 1400s, but officially in 1535, the history of the islands changed its course forever. Pirates and whalers discovered giant tortoises there that could survive on little or nothing for months. They piled as many as six hundred at a time into the holds of their ships— with neither food nor water—and ate them on their long voyages, lasting a year sometimes. With more systematic destruction, later seafarers took the docile iguanas for food and seals for fur. And, inadvertently or otherwise, they introduced animals, such as rats and goats and cats, which devastated native life until many species were "erased from the list of living things."

In 1835, Charles Darwin, a young medical-school dropout and highly uninspired divinity student, visited the islands aboard the HMS *Beagle* on a historic journey that, for better or worse, "put them on the map." As an unpaid observer (and the captain's second choice, at that), he collected specimens and recorded his observations. These islands so haunted him following his brief stay there that from them, years later, he was able to develop his theory of evolution by natural selection, a monument in scientific thought.

The future of the Galápagos is uncertain. The government of Ecuador, which owns them, and groups such as the Charles Darwin Foundation are doing what they can to preserve this place for study—toward discoveries we cannot yet imagine; and for people to witness Nature's splendor. Still, the increasing number of people there (tourists, locals, fishermen) threatens the wildlife and the islands themselves. The plunder of the animals goes on—of sea cucumbers, of turtles, of sharks, all for food; and of small, less-noticed things.

After reading about them for a lifetime, in 1995 I visited the Galápagos. When you stand in this place, wild and vast and stark, looking out over the endless and shining skin of the sea, you hear the flutter and roar of Creation, feel the stir of your own beginnings upon the delicate chain of life. Here, you are at the core of the mystery and poetry of Nature.

These islands symbolize the peril that the entire earth faces. We can take it apart, sea turtle by sea turtle, shell by shell, but we cannot put it back together.

Meanwhile, as we struggle with our humanity, the sun bakes their old backs, the wind caresses the salt grass, the waves wash the Galápagos.